**Disney · PIXAR**

# TOY STORY

# READY, SET, DRAW!

A GOLDEN BOOK • NEW YORK

ISBN: 978-0-7364-2728-9
www.randomhouse.com/kids
Printed in the United States of America
10 9 8 7 6 5 4 3 2

Andy loves to play cowboy games with Woody.
Draw a cowboy hat for each of them.

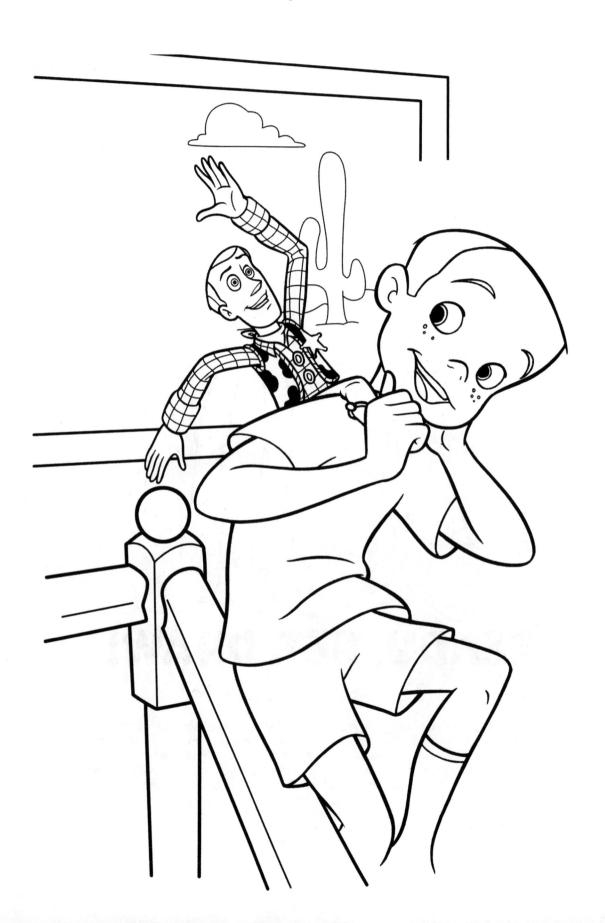

Rex and Hamm are Andy's toys.
Draw Rex's tail and Hamm's legs.

Slinky is a loyal dog.
Draw the coils that help him stretch.

Woody is sitting in his special spot.
Finish Andy's bed.

# Woody calls a meeting!
## Draw a microphone for him to talk into.

Rex is a T. rex!
Draw some more blocks for him to knock over.

Bo Peep has lost her sheep.
Draw some sheep for her to find.

Hamm is a piggy bank.
Draw some more coins for him to keep safe.

# It's Andy's birthday!
## Draw a pile of presents for him to open.

Woody is spying on the new toy in Andy's room.
Draw the blanket that Woody is hiding under.

Buzz Lightyear is a space ranger.
Draw his helmet and the buttons on his suit.

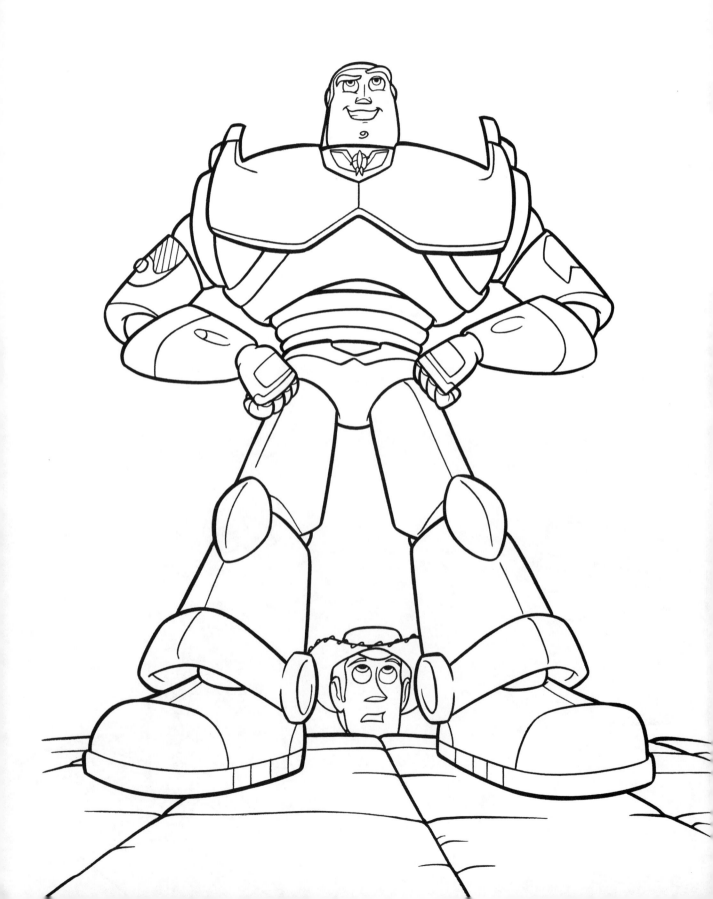

# Where is Buzz flying to?
## Use your imagination to complete this scene.

Andy loves to play with Buzz.
Draw Andy a space helmet to match Buzz's.

Buzz has fallen out Andy's window!
Draw some bushes for him to land on.

Buzz hitches a ride!
Draw his getaway car.

Buzz and Woody are lost!
Draw a Pizza Planet truck to rescue them.

Buzz and Woody sneak into Pizza Planet
disguised as a shake and a burger.
Draw their legs poking out of each disguise.

Fill the Rocket Ship Crane Game with more toy Aliens.

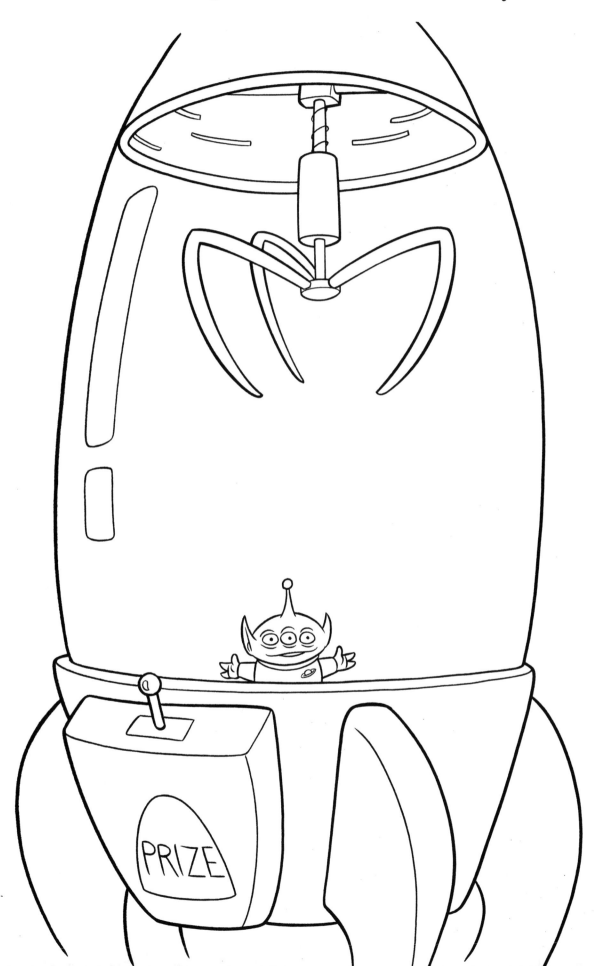

Buzz and Woody have been chosen!
Draw the Claw that lifts them out of the game.

Sid is happy that he won Buzz and Woody.
Draw a smile on his face.

Buzz and Woody are frightened!
Draw some creepy shadows around them.

Sid's mutant toys are scary!
Draw some parts to complete each one.

What does Buzz see on TV?
Complete the scene to show what he's watching.

Buzz is at a tea party! Draw a teacup for him.

Sid has gotten a package! Draw what was inside the box.

Buzz is sad.
Draw a frown on his face.

Woody has a plan! Draw the map that he is working on.

Woody is in charge now!
Draw the sheriff's badge on Woody's vest.

## What spooked Sid?
## Draw it.

Sid runs away.
Draw some more mutant toys around him.

Buzz and Woody are friends now.
Draw them shaking hands.

Andy misses his favorite toys.
Draw a cowboy hat and a spaceship in his hands.

Buzz and Woody are free!
Finish the fence they just climbed through.

Buzz and Woody are running as fast as they can!
Draw the moving truck they are chasing.

Oh, no! Draw a rope for Woody to hold on to.

Draw some toys that Andy has packed in this moving box.

RC comes to the rescue!
Draw the remote control that Woody is using to steer.

Buzz and Woody are flying! Draw Buzz's wings.

Andy has found his favorite toys!
Draw Buzz and Woody in the box.

Buzz and Woody are happy to be back with Andy.
Draw a smile on Andy's face.

Buzz Lightyear is a space ranger!
Draw his wings and his spaceship.

Buzz and Woody are good friends.
Draw some other toys around them.

Buzz and Woody give each other a high five!
Draw their hands.

What are the toys watching?
Draw what's on the screen.

Rex loves video games!
Draw a remote control so he can play.

What does Woody see out the window?
Complete the scene to show what he's looking at.

# Woody has found Wheezy!
## Draw Wheezy's bow tie.

Woody is at a yard sale!
Draw some things that are for sale.

Al is stealing Woody!
Draw Woody's cowboy hat.

# Buzz chases Al's car! Draw the car.

Woody makes new friends!
Draw the boxes they jumped out of.

Woody meets another toy.
Draw a box around the Prospector.

Woody likes to watch *Woody's Roundup* on TV!
Draw the TV he's looking at.

Woody is getting painted.
Draw the brush that the Cleaner is using.

Jessie and Woody have a chat.
Draw what Jessie is talking about.

Jessie is a rootin', tootin' cowgirl!
Draw her cowgirl hat, and add a bandanna
around her neck.

Draw a big chicken in front of Al's Toy Barn.

Buzz leads the other toys on a rescue mission to find Woody. Draw traffic cones over Slinky and Rex to help them hide as they cross the street.

Rex and Hamm explore Al's Toy Barn.
Draw shelves full of toys around them.

Rex wants to learn how to defeat Emperor Zurg.
Decorate the video game manual Rex is reading.

Hamm, Rex, and Slinky go for a ride.
Draw the car they're cruising in.

Buzz Lightyear discovers a brand-new Buzz Lightyear toy!
Draw the box the toy is in.

New Buzz has captured the real Buzz!
Draw New Buzz's wings and backpack.

Al is calling a museum owner in Japan.
Draw a phone for Al.

Andy's toys find a hiding place.
Finish the bag they sneak into.

Buzz hides from the evil Emperor Zurg!
Draw Zurg.

Jessie loves critters!
Draw some animals for her to rescue.

# Slinky meets the Prospector.
# Draw the Prospector's hat.

Woody misses Andy.
Draw a little boy who looks like Andy on the TV.

# Draw the Prospector's pick.

Buzz is running from falling asteroids.
Draw the asteroids.

# What are Andy's toys trying to reach?
## Draw it.

Buzz is searching for Woody at the airport!
Draw some luggage on the conveyor belts.

Woody is trapped!
Finish drawing the string the Prospector
used to tie Woody up.

The toys blind the Prospector with camera flashes.
Draw the cameras they are using.

The Prospector gets a new home.
Draw some other dolls in the backpack.

Jessie is trapped in a suitcase!
Draw the bag she is in on the conveyor belt.

Buzz and Bullseye help Woody chase Jessie's plane.
Draw the plane.

Woody opens a suitcase and finds Jessie!
Finish the suitcase.

# What do Woody and Jessie see?
## Draw it.

Buzz tries to catch Woody's hat.
Draw the hat flying toward him.

Woody and Jessie get off the plane safely!
Draw the plane taking off into the sky.

Andy loves to make Buzz fly!
Draw the galaxy he is flying through.

Andy pretends the Roundup gang is in the desert.
Draw some cactuses around them.

# Draw a spaceship for the Aliens.

Sheriff Woody walks through the desert.
Draw his boots.

Jessie rides to the rescue!
Draw her hat and braid trailing behind her.

Buzz Lightyear lifts a moving train!
Draw some train cars above him.

Slinky has captured some bandits.
Draw his coils around them to hold them in place.

It's the evil Dr. Porkchop!
Draw a control panel in front of him.

Andy is all grown up.
Draw some posters on his walls.

Buzz watches the Green Army Men jump out the window.
Draw their parachutes.

Woody watches as Andy's mom picks up
a bag full of Andy's toys.
Draw the bag she is about to take out to the curb.

Woody has to free his friends
before the garbage truck arrives!
Draw the truck driving up the street.

Buzz and Jessie need Rex's tail to tear open the bag.
Draw Rex's pointy tail.

Andy's toys decide to go to Sunnyside Daycare.
Draw the donation box that they climb into.

The toys meet Lotso the stuffed bear at Sunnyside.
Draw Lotso's cane.

Slinky and Hamm meet Stretch.
Draw all eight of her tentacles.

Jessie meets a jack-in-the-box.
Draw his hat.

The Aliens spot a claw!
Draw the Claw above them.

Rex makes new friends. Draw some more dinosaurs.

Big Baby needs his bottle.
Draw it in his hand before he starts to cry.

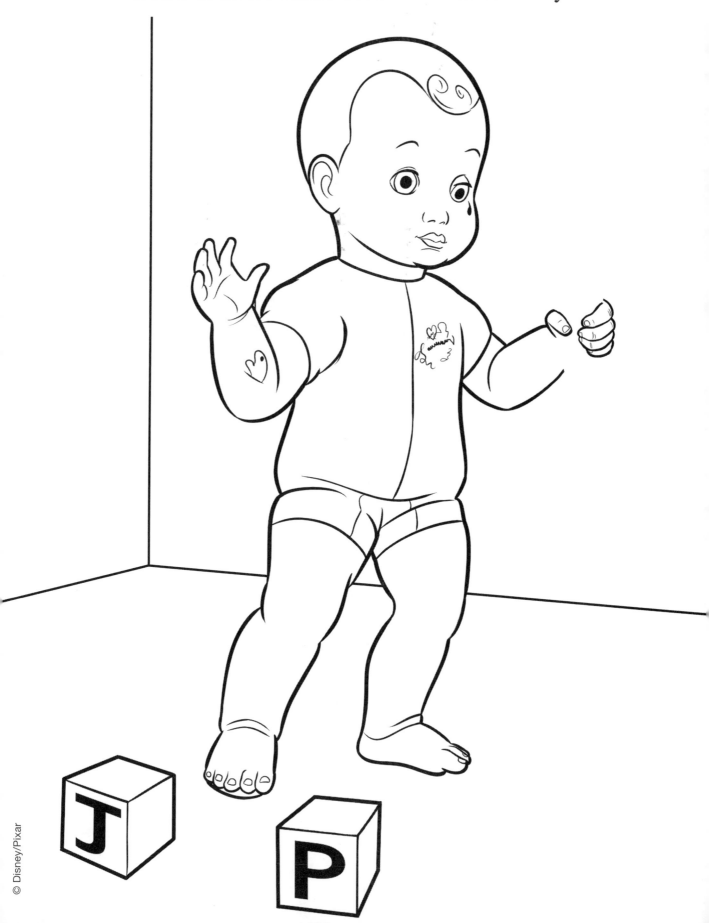

Woody needs to fly out of Sunnyside.
Draw a kite for him to hold on to.

This little girl likes to hammer.
Decorate her paper crown.

This little girl uses Jessie as a paintbrush.
Draw the mess she has made with her paints.

Jessie tries to escape from Sunnyside.
Draw the door she is trying to open.

# Draw a rope for Buzz to climb.

Lotso wants to study Buzz's instruction manual.
Draw what's on the cover.

Woody needs a place to hide.
Finish the backpack he is climbing into.

Bullseye is especially happy when Woody returns.
Draw Bullseye's wagging tail.

The toys sneak past Big Baby.
Finish Big Baby's swing.

Woody finds the heart charm that used to belong to Lotso.
Finish the charm in his hand.

© Disney/Pixar

# Big Baby is going to throw Lotso in the Dumpster!
## Draw the Dumpster.

# The toys get dumped!
## Draw the pile of trash that breaks their fall.

Jessie and Rex hold on tight!
Draw what is below them.

The toys run!
Draw what you think they are running from.

Only Lotso can shut down
the conveyor belt and save the toys.
Draw the button he must press.

The Aliens use the Claw to save their friends!
Draw the Aliens in the control tower.

The three Aliens cheer!
Draw one more Alien to complete the scene.

Lotso has a new home.
Finish the garbage truck he is stuck to.

Woody helps Hamm clean up.
Draw the hose he uses as a shower.

Buzz and Woody prepare to say goodbye.
Draw some boxes in the background.

Woody must write a very important note.
Draw a pencil for him to use.

Bonnie loves toys.
Draw some toys for her to play with.

Andy introduces Bonnie to his favorite toy.
Draw Bonnie's happy face.

Andy and Bonnie have fun playing together.
Draw a sun and some clouds above them.

Buzz and Woody say goodbye to Andy.
Draw Andy's car pulling away.